You Make Me

Crazy

You Make Me Crazy

Portia Devonshire

For my one and only little sister,

Happy 18th year around the sun
May your present forever remind you that I am here to embarrass you

Originally drafted as a fanfiction for her while she was in primary school, and I was in high school. Until it was officially published, she had not read it.

2025

Contents

Trigger Warnings

- Bullying[1]
- Child Murder, Adult Murder, Child Sexual Assault (all happen off page but are explained on page
- Verbal Abuse
- Emotional Abuse

Helplines for Children & Young People[2]

Lifeline
0800 543 354
Free text 4357 (HELP)

Youthline
0800 376 633
Free text 234

Whats Up (For 5 - 18-year-olds)
Phone counselling is available every day
11am - 11pm
0800 942 8787
Online Chat
11am - 10:30 pm
https://whatsup.co.nz/

---

[1] Find out more about what is classified as bullying in New Zealand head to
www.govt.nz/browse/law-crime-and-justice/abuse-harassment-domestic-violence/bullying/
[2] For more help or information head to
https://mentalhealth.org.nz/help/ or https://bullyingfree.nz/

Mollie's POV

I'm the normal sort of girl, stuck in one of those lame-ass high schools. I have dirty blonde hair that falls in a curtain to my shoulders and intriguing hazel eyes to match. I could be classed as a nerd if anyone asked me, I don't wear glasses like the stereotypical nerd does and I'm certainly not popular or well-loved by all the boys like the cheerleaders are. I'm usually found listening to music or reading. I'm the quiet type of girl. My name is Mollie, but my friends call my Monster.

I walk down the corridor, heading towards my next class. I take a left into a shadowed doorway and nearly walk into a group of guys all hanging out by the door. I recognize Drew Martin after another glance at them. The rest of the group remains a mystery to me.

My best friend, Jemma walks into class after me, walking straight into me as her attention is on the group of mystery boys,
"OMG Mollie," She squeals in my ear as she jumps up and down on the spot. "You are never going to guess what I have to tell you."
"Calm down Jemma, what is it this time?" I asked, rolling my eyes. She is always gossiping about something.
"ARE YOU FREAKING SERIOUS MOLLIE!" she yells at me, looking at me like I'm stupid.

"What's the big deal? Drew Martin and five new guys are in our class," I say, pulling out the book I need for this class.

"Monster, those five super-hot guys are Four Singers and a Casket!" she exclaims. I groan hearing the band name. She is constantly rambling on about them and how 'great' their music is.
"You know I don't care for them, Jem. We don't share the same taste in music." I can see she is practically bouncing in her seat wanting to talk about it, however.
"Fine, you can talk about it," I let out a deep sigh.

Her face lights up instantly and a giant smile spread across her face. "Well, the one that is standing closest to the teacher's desk and looks as cute as a button with the perfect hair is Lucas," she begins her word vomit. I make a gagging sound in response. His hair is what I envision Muffin McClay would look like. "The one with the ear piercing and the tattoos peeking out from under his sleeves is Zaid." she points to the one wearing a flannel that reminds me of a lumberjack. "The blonde one by the door is Declan. He has a super-hot accent," she sighs like a lovestruck maiden. "And the one standing next to him in the green shirt is Troy. He is my favourite."

"Thanks for that useless information, did you do the homework?" I ask opening my book.

You Make Me Crazy

"I can't believe you're changing the subject when the five hottest guys and Drew Martin are in our class! But yes I did complete it," she shakes her head at me. "Come on, class is about to start. We can talk afterwards, I really need to study," I said as the teacher walked into class.

"Good morning class" our teacher, Mrs. Dammers walks into the classroom, "This morning we have six new students to welcome into the class." she puts her bag on her chair and turns to the group of boys at the front. "These are Drew, Lucas, Declan, James, Zaid and Troy." All the girls in the class suddenly start to excitedly whisper to each other. All the guys in the class grunt hello or hi to the group. "Do your best to be nice to them," Mrs. Dammers says as she turns to the whiteboard.

I am thankful when the bell finally rings. Having to spend an entire class listening to people constantly whisper and pass notes when you are trying to pay attention to the lesson is annoying. I pack my stuff up so quickly that Jemma is struggling to keep up as I practically run out of the room. I rush to my safe spot in the library, a quiet corner in a section that most people don't go into.

Taking a seat at the familiar table, I begin to sort my lunch out. A large shadow creeps its way over the table towards me. "Surely no one wants to be in a library so badly that they run out of class," a male voice speaks to me. I look up from my lunch, my eyes landing on Drew Martin's.

"What do you want Drew?" I ask with a mouth full of food.

"How attractive Mollie, or should I say Monster?" he sits across from me.

"Don't make me repeat myself, Martin," I warn.

"Monster it is then," he chuckles, "You've made it rather clear that you're not interested in me or the boys,"

"Remind me again what little playgroup your 'boys' are a part of."

"Very funny. We are both aware you know what Four Singers and a Casket is. Your little friend wouldn't shut up about them."

"You leave her out of this," I cut in.

"I have a proposition for you." he entwines his fingers in front of himself on the table.

"What does it involve me doing?" I ask, raising an eyebrow at him.

"Nothing overly different than you already are, just with the boys and I."

"Why on earth would I want to do that?" he ignores my question and continues talking.

"After we've been friends for a bit, I will give you another task."

"What's in it for me?" he raises two fingers.

"We can make you famous," he wiggles one finger, "You can get paid $5,000 a week," he wiggles the other finger, "Or you can have both," he wiggles both fingers.

I give it a long hard think before looking at him.

You Make Me Crazy

"Pay starts today." I take another bite of my food.
"I knew you would come round to it." he gets up and straightens his shirt, "Nice talking to you Monster." I pull the middle finger at his back as he walks away from me.

I woke up early the next morning, lying in bed and pondering on the event yesterday, in the library. Dragging myself out of bed, I walk over to my bathroom and get ready for the day. I don my usual clothing choices. Shorts, tight shirt and a letterman jacket. I hug it slightly, remembering how it used to be my brothers.

Downstairs, I can hear mum talking to someone in the kitchen. I rush down the stairs to find Drew and my mum sitting at the table together, having a conversation,
"Drew, what are you doing here?" I asked, surprised to see him.
"I'm here to pick you up for school love," he said, pulling out his car keys.
"Mother, you let him in here? What the hell were you thinking?" I accused her.

"Darling, your lovely boyfriend came to pick you up for school. You should be nicer, it's very kind of him," my mother says, 'oh so calmly'.
"HE ISN'T MY BOYFRIEND!" I yell at her, getting frustrated. "Come on Drew, we're going," I grab an apple from the fruit bowl, snatching my bag off the floor and rushing out the door.

I get outside and wait by Drew's car for him. He walks

out the door yelling 'Goodbye' to my mother. "Hop in the car babe," he smirks, opening my door for me.

"Oh, such a gentleman," I reply, my voice full of sarcasm because I am still pissed at him. As we drive the short distance to school, Drew tries to make conversation with me.

"Babe, be happy."

"Don't call me 'babe' Drew, I am not your girlfriend."

"For the deal to work and for you to become famous, one of us six handsome guys is going to be your boyfriend."

"Well it won't be you. None of you guys are handsome anyway. Just let me get to know the others and if that's what it takes, then fine!" I huff. We pull up to the school with everyone staring at us as Drew acts the gentleman and opens my door for me, offering me his hand to help me out.

I run off to class yelling 'bye' and 'thank you' over my shoulder to Drew, rushing down the hall until I reach my class. Since I am still running, I don't notice the class door is open, and I collide straight into a 'brick wall'.

"Miss are you okay?" the 'brick wall' asks me, holding me up.

"Sorry. I wasn't watching where I was going, I didn't see you there," I apologise.

"It's okay. It's nice to meet you, I'm Zaid," the 'brick wall', Zaid introduces himself.

"Oh, I'm Mollie, but everyone calls me 'Monster'. You're one of the Four Singers and a Casket boy's aren't you?" I ask, holding my books to my chest.

"That's me," he confirms, "You're not one of those weird fans are you? I would like to make friends here and they make it really hard to find someone genuine,"
"I am not a weird fan," I reassured him.
"Great," he smiles at me, "We can be friends then, if that's something you're cool with?"

The deal I made with Drew pops into my head.
"I guess we can be friends. What about your other band buddies?" I ask.
"They'll love having a friend to hang out with."
"I guess that settles it then," I smile at him.
"Hey, you were sitting next to that Jemma girl yesterday, weren't you?"
"Jemma's my best friend,"
"Great! You can bring her along when we hang out. Troy has a bit of a crush on her."
"Okay," I said smiling. "Now if you wouldn't mind getting out of my way, I need to get to class."
"Let me walk you to your seat," he offers.
"Sure,"

Zaid walks me to my seat and then sits next to me, getting his books out. I see Jemma walk into class and glare at me. She stops and stands for a brief moment before walking for a while before coming over to me.
"Zaid, you must have some balls to take MY seat next to

MY best friend," she growls at him, making him jump in his seat.

"You should move," I suggest.

"But I was sitting here first, and I want to sit next to Monster," he argues, banging his hands on the desk like a three-year-old, not getting his own way.

I lightly slap him across the back of the head. He looks over at me and mutters, "That hurt," rubbing the back of his head.

"Toughen up, I thought you were a man," I say, pushing him out of his seat.

Jemma quickly sits down in the vacant chair, "What a gentleman, thank you, Zaid." I watch him as he walks off mumbling under his breath. "Monster!" Jemma exclaims, "You were sitting next to a famous person. OMG!" she squeals.

"Yeah, Drew Martin picked me up from home this morning too. Oh, and while I remember, we're going to hang out with them at lunch," I tell her.

"OMG!" she screams, deafening me.

"Jemma!" I scolded her. Everyone in the class is looking at us strangely. Zaid and Lucas seem to be sharing a quiet laugh.

I am relieved when the bell rings at the end of class. I am the first one out of the door and into the corridor. Walking fast so no one can catch me. I almost ran to Health, my favourite class at school.

You Make Me Crazy

Sitting down at my seat at the back of the class, I pull out my iPod and headphones. I never get caught listening to music in this class as the teacher is actually my older cousin, Heather.

I turned up the volume blasting 'Monster' by Jay-Z and Kanye West. I watched as everyone began to fill the classroom. To my surprise, Drew and James walk in and take both the desks either side of me.

"You shouldn't listen to music in class," James comments, pulling out one of my headphones. I give him an icy glare.
"Leave me and my music alone," I snapped. "Heather doesn't care."
"Who's Heather?" Drew asks. Oblivious that I was talking about the teacher. "Do you mean Miss Matheson?" James chimes in.
"Yes Miss Matheson as you call her," I reply sarcastically,
"Why do you call her Heather?" they both question me at once. "Because I can, duh! But that doesn't mean you can."

Just then, my cousin walks into class, James looks at her and starts drooling. I laugh as the drool starts to make its way down the front of his shirt. Heather has long brown hair that bounces around her shoulders and has baby crystal blue eyes that shine.

I nudge Drew in the ribs and silently point at James. He cracks up laughing, snapping James out of his drool fest.

"Man you're in love," Drew says between laughs.

"Am not!" James shoots back.

"Drew's right James, there's no denying it. The look on your face and the drool running down your shirt says so," I laugh.

"Oh shut up," he mumbles, folding his arms and lying his head on his desk.

Miss Matheson walks down to the back of the room once she has handed out the work. She stood next to James's desk and spoke. "Well, you two must be the new guys, James and Drew. I'm Miss Matheson, it's nice to have you in my class."

"Oh and M, here's money for lunch," she hands me $20.

"Thanks, want me to get you anything?" I ask, tucking the money into my pocket.

"No, it's okay, you just keep the new boys happy at lunch," she says walking off back to the front of the class.

"I don't believe it," Drew marvels, resting his head in his hands. "The teacher just gave you lunch money!" James mutters in awe.

"So?" I question them.

"That's not normal," James challenges.

"You're idiots," I chuckle.

"Miss Matheson, or as I call her Heather, is my cousin.

You Make Me Crazy

She is my father's brother's daughter. I'm surprised you didn't get that since we have the same last name,"

"Oh," James breathes before asking "Do you think I would have a chance with her?"
"Like I said he's in love," Drew mutters.
"Maybe," I said, getting up from my chair and grabbing my bag. "Come on, the bell rung and I'm starving," I told them walking out of the room.

Sitting at our table in the cafe, Jemma and I start stuffing our faces with food when the boys come over and sit with us.
"What are you doing here?" Jemma snaps, not liking the death stares girls are sending us.
"Oh, you know, just sitting and eating," Declan responds casually, while taking a massive bite out of his sandwich.
"Wow! Someone's brave enough to come sit with us after what happened this morning," I said, taunting Zaid. "Not afraid it's going to happen again?"
"Nope," he replies, grinning like a crazy person.

"What happened this morning?" Troy asks curiously.
"I was bullied, a little," Zaid mumbles.
"Yeah, by girls," I giggle while eating my lunch.
"You got bullied by girls?!" Lucas asks, almost laughing.
"Yeah..." Zaid replies cautiously.
"What girls?" Declan demands.
"Monster and Jemma," Zaid says in a near whisper.

"What did you say? Mollie and Jemma?" Drew looks at us with a questioning look.

"Hey! He stole my seat, he deserved it," Jemma defends herself. Lucas, Declan, Troy and James look at Zaid.
"You took a girl's seat? How classic!" James gives Zaid a hard pat on the back.
"So what?" Zaid asks annoyed.
"Zaid, you never take a girl's seat," Drew responds.
Zaid gives a loud huff before getting up and stomping his way out of the room.
"Well, I think he overreacted a little," Troy says, taking a bite of his burger.

"'A little' is an understatement. Someone should go after him," Declan says with slight concern.
"Bags not!" Lucas, Troy, James, Drew and Jemma grumbled.
"Fine I will," I say grumpily getting up out of my seat.
"Don't do anything I wouldn't do," Jemma calls out to me.
"And what's that? You would do everything," I call back to her over my shoulder.
"Exactly," everyone at the table making kissy noises behind me.

I walk out of the lunch room doors muttering about how immature everyone is, when I see Zaid slumped down on the ground by my locker. I walk over to him and slowly sit down next to him. "You okay?" I asked, leaning my head on his shoulder.

13

"Yeah, what do you want?" he asks in a huff. It doesn't seem like he wants me here.

"I wanted to see if you're okay," I reply honestly.

I sit with him in silence as a tear slowly makes its way down his cheek. I wrap my arms around his neck and pull him into me for a close hug. He hesitates briefly before wrapping his arms around me and pulling us tightly together.

"Thank you," he whispers into my hair.

"It's okay," I responded.

"There's something I want to tell you," he says quietly into my neck.

"Yeah, what is it?" I relaxed at the touch of his lips on my neck.

"I really like you," he whispers.

"I like you too," I say as we pull away from each other. He looks really worried.

"I know we've only known each other for a short while, but I was wondering if you would be my girlfriend? There is just something about you that feels right," he asked, looking serious.

"Yes," I reply instantly. A massive smile grows on his face as he leans in close to kiss me again.

I hear a throat clear behind me, the two of us pulling away to see who it is. I look around and find the others staring at us. Jemma's mouth is wide open.

"You are so lucky! You had your first kiss with a famous person," Jemma squeals making everyone block their ears. Zaid wraps his arms around my waist. Damn! He's possessive already.

"Yeah, so how's that a big deal?" he asks. Before she can answer, I butt in.

"She hasn't been kissed yet," I say, watching her blush beetroot red.

"I told you not to tell anyone that and you promised you wouldn't!" she growls angrily.

"I'm sorry," I said to her sadly.

I watch Troy walk behind her and grab her shoulders, twirls her around and plants one on her lips. Sitting there I start giggling as Lucas, James, Declan and Drew groaned in disgust, Zaid just rests his head on my shoulder causing me to snuggle back into him more. Troy pulls back slowly and smiles, letting Jemma collapse in his arms.

"Well, I guess now there's only four of us left." Drew chuckles.

"But only one of you is dating someone?" Jemma questions.

"Actually," Troy starts blushing, "that kiss was my way of asking you out."

"Oh," Jemma replies, blushing harder. "So, it is only four of you now."

Everyone starts laughing as the bell rings. "Babe, I'll meet you at the front of the school at the end of the day, to take you home," Zaid says, kissing my cheek.

"But I thought Drew was taking you home?" Jemma

asks, confused. "Nah it's fine. I only brought her to school," Drew jumps in calmly putting his hands into his pockets.

"I'm going to class. Who's coming?"

"Let's go," I say, grabbing Jemma's hand and pulling her to class.

"See you boys after school," she calls over her shoulder, blowing Troy a kiss. Giggling, we walk off to class.

I am walking out of class towards the front of the school when I feel arms wrap around my waist and pull me to the side of the school. I slap my 'kidnapper' across the face before I turn to see it's Drew. "Crap Drew. What's this about? I'm meant to be meeting up with Zaid," I yell at him.

"I just wanted to tell you that now you're dating Zaid and Jemma is dating Troy, you are both going to become 'famous'. Are you up with it?" he asks, rubbing the spot where I slapped him.

"Yes, now I have somewhere to be," I run off towards the gate where I find Zaid. I run up to him and jump onto his back, "Hey," I yell in his ear, giggling.

"Hey babe," he pulls me off his back into his arms and hugs me tight.

"Can we go now?" I asked, slightly impatient.

"Sure, I hope you don't mind that I ride and not drive," he says, gesturing towards the bike next to us.

"Wow!" I exclaim, almost yelling in excitement. "I love it, can we go now?" I beg him.

Mollie's POV

"Sure," he hands me a spare helmet helping me onto the back of the bike. We zoom off home.

Walking into the living room after being dropped off by Zaid, I flop down onto the couch and fall asleep. I wake up to a cold glass of water being tipped on my head.

Looking for the culprit I see my mother standing over me. "Get up," she growls. "You have to hurry and get ready for school, a boy is here for you," she says grumpily.

I jump up and race to the kitchen, grabbing an apple before sprinting to my room. Rummaging through my drawers while taking bites from the apple, I pull out a pair of tight red jeans and a flowy black shirt. Dumping my apple core in the bin, I jump into the shower, quickly getting cleaned and dried. After fixing my hair, teeth shoes and clothes I waltz back into the kitchen.

My mother and Zaid are sitting at the table together. Damn this reminds me of yesterday when Drew was here. "Who is this boy?" my mother asks, sounding strongly disappointed in me.
"Mother, this is Zaid Yousuf. He's my boyfriend and from the musical singing group Four Singers and a Casket. My friend Jemma is going out with Troy Thompson. Drew Martin, who was here yesterday, is just a friend of mine," I explain.

"Oh," she says quietly "I thought you were two-timing that lovely boy Drew."

"Mrs Matheson, I would never go after one of my closest friends' girlfriends. I'm not like that, I respect people and their relationships." Zaid pipes up.

"I can see that now," my mother smiles, "and please call me Grace. Mrs Matheson was Mollie's grandmother and her aunty."

"Okay Grace. Come on, Mollie, we better start making our way to school," Zaid smiles standing up, putting an arm around me as we walk to the door.

"Let's go, I have to talk to Heather," I say, hopping on the bike behind him.

"Why do you call her 'Heather' and not 'Miss Matheson?" he asks before quickly adding, "She is family isn't she?"

"Yup," I answer as we speed off on his bike.

At school, I jump off the bike and kiss his cheek. "I'm going to go find Heather, you go find the boys. I'll see you in class or at lunch," I say, starting to walk off.

"Wait, can I come with you?" Zaid asks, grabbing my arm.

"Sure okay," I respond, linking my arm with his.

When we arrive at her classroom, I quickly look through the door window before opening it. I find James is in her classroom with her. Heather is spread out on her back across a table while James makes himself at home between her legs. I pull Zaid away from the door before he can see what's going on inside.

18

Mollie's POV

"Hey, I thought you wanted to go see your cousin," Zaid asks, pulling me to a halt.
"She was busy. I forgot she told me she was doing extra help for catch up classes; Wednesday mornings," I lie, not wanting to tell him I saw James and Heather together.
"Who was in there?" Zaid asks, seeing straight through my lie.
"James and my cousin," I mumble. Zaid chuckles.
"I'm glad he has managed to score himself some loving. I was wondering how long it was going to take him. But I must say if they do get serious it's a good thing that it's our last year of school." I giggle quietly agreeing with him.
"Come on, let's go to class," Zaid says, wrapping his arm around my waist, pulling me along beside him towards our next class.

The school day goes by quickly, which I was thankful for as I absolutely don't like the hell hole they call school. I am at home sitting at the kitchen table with homework covering it and music blasting from the speakers in the lounge.it takes me a minute to hear the loud knocking on the door. Damn whoever it is, couldn't they have interrupted me at a better time? I get up and walk over to the door, a scowl on my face. I yank the door open quickly. I find Drew standing outside my house with a manilla folder in his hands saying 'Deal Agreements' in bright red capitals. This doesn't look good.

James' POV

I pull up outside of Mollie's driveway just after Drew has gotten out of the car holding a Manilla file under his arm. It looks like something serious but for now I'll keep my nose out of it since it has nothing to do with me. It's probably just some school project, I'll fall asleep reading the description of. I keep an eye on the front door as I pull out of her driveway. Mollie opens the big front door with a scowl on her face. She doesn't look happy at all to see Martin. Driving off, my phone begins to ring and when I check the caller identification, Zaid's name flashes across the screen. I pick it up using the handsfree.

"What's up?" I ask.

"I'm bored out of my mind and want to see Mollie, but I have no ride," he replies.

"I just dropped Drew off at her place," I say without thinking. "He looked like he meant business."

"YOU LEFT MOLLIE ALONE WITH HIM!" Zaid yells through the phone.

"Ahh w-well yes?" I stutter, more or less questioning my own choices.

"YOU IDIOT," he roars at me "YOU KNOW HE HAS A REPUTATION FOR STEALING OTHER GUYS GIRL! I WANT YOU TO GET BACK THERE NOW AND TELL HIM SOMETHING THAT WILL MAKE HIM LEAVE!

"I'm truly sorry man I wasn't thinking," I start apologizing, turning the car around just as Zaid hangs up on me. I see Drew on the side of the road walking towards me, so I pull over to let him in.

Mollie's POV

I let out a breath I didn't know I was holding as Drew finally leaves my house, after explaining what he asked me to do. And if I hadn't done it, my dearest mother, sister and cousin would pay. I can't let that happen to them after losing my father. I walk into the kitchen to make myself something to eat. Once I'm done forcing the food down my throat, I take myself off to bed not caring that it's only seven pm. I need to sleep this off and hope it's all just a dream. I grab the files Drew left on the table and walk up to my room, dumping them on the to draw of the bedside table.

I wake up early and drag myself out of bed. What Drew said, still fresh in my mind, apparently my plan to sleep it away didn't work. Lazily, I drag myself to the shower. Although it is only Thursday, I don't want to deal with the rest of the week.. Turning the shower on, I get in. Drew's words run through my mind. *"The closer you get to them, the more it's going to hurt… don't forget that if you fail, your family will get the blame… you really don't even like him!"*

After getting frustrated with his words, I slam the shower off. I dry myself off quickly and almost sprint to get dressed. I pull on the first thing I can find and ran to grab a peach, before leaving to walk to school.

21

Arriving at school, I keep my head low in hopes that I wouldn't be noticed by the guys. I see Jemma with them and our eyes suddenly meet. She can tell by my posture that I want to be left alone. I get to my locker without being recognised. As I file through my books for the next class, I hear a throat clear behind me. Turning around, I came face to face with Zaid, who has a hurt expression on his face.

"Hey, you okay?" I ask quietly, reaching my hand out. Just as I am about to softly touch his face, he pulls away from my hand.
"Why was he at your place yesterday afternoon?" Zaid demands angrily. Instantly I know who he means.
"It's okay babe he only wanted to give me some files. He explained them to me and then I kicked him out," I answer before turning to shut my locker.
"Oh," he says quietly. "I thought he was there for something else, I'm sorry."
"It's okay," I reassure him, stretching up on my tip toes to peck his cheek.
"Let me walk you to class," he offers his arm out to me.

The school day goes by quickly which I am glad of. I get home and go straight to my room, taking out the files from my draw. Looking over them I see who is first - Lucas.
I read over his profile information.

```
Name: Lucas Walker
Common Hang-Out: Fishnets Bar
Location: 3/7 Redtint Road
Deadline: Saturday
```

I ponder for a while when I come to realise I have no idea where the bar is. I pull out my laptop to search it up. It turns out to be a strip bar 20-minute walk from my house. I decide it is going to be a Friday night girls night out.

I read through more of the information Martin has left me, and find out I have some people to go see tomorrow. It looks like I wouldn't be going to school tomorrow at all, not that it bothers me.

After finishing my homework, I send a text to Jemma telling her we should have a girls night out tomorrow and that I won't be at school. Before I know it I get a text back confirming that she'll come with me.

I wake up late, but I didn't care, I was taking a day off anyway. After going downstairs, I find a note mum has left on the table for me.

Mollie,

I am working today and then going to my friend June's place for the night.

Lots of love,

Mum

You Make Me Crazy

P.S Don't be home alone with your boyfriend.

I make pancakes with chocolate chips and blueberries before settling down to devour them. Tossing the dishes into the sink, I go to get ready. After showering, I run through my checklist. Tight black leather pants. Check. Black wife beater. Check. Black leather jacket. Check. Leather combat boots. Check. Dark black make-up with straightened hair. Check.

I pick up my phone, slide it into my jacket pocket, grab my wallet, take out my cards and cash, and slip them into my pockets. I grab my iPod shuffle and clip it to my belt, putting the buds in my ears. I shuffle through my music to find a song to my liking - Highway To Hell. I run down the stairs, and all I can hear is the buckles on my combats. Running to the front door, I grab the piece of paper and take my keys. Going outside, I lock the door and walk off towards my first destination, Carly's.

When I arrive at the place Drew told me I needed to go to, I repeat the instructions that were written in the file. I need to find someone who is named Carl. When I find him, I am to tell him a code word to prove who I am. After that, he will give me a duffle bag full of equipment that I need to complete the next task Drew has told me about.

I knock on the door, shyness and nervousness filling my body. Slowly the door opens, and a gruff voice speaks.

Mollie's POV

"And what do you have?" the man asks. I know this is the first part of the code.

"I have five wild geese and a swan to be tamed," I respond. On the way here, I was trying to figure out what the phrase meant.

Then I realise the five wild geese are Zaid, Declan, Lucas, James and Troy and that the swan was Drew. "Here," the gruff voiced man says, sticking a black duffle bag out the door, still keeping himself hidden. "Don't open it until you get home. It's all safe but if a citizen sees it, the police will come knocking," he warns.

I take the duffle bag and walk away. As soon as the bus arrives, I get on and go straight home. When I get through the door I check the time. It is already 4 o'clock, it took me 4 hours, from waking up to walking through the door just now.

I run upstairs and put the bag on my bed before checking my phone. I have a text from Jemma, saying she will pick me up at 7. I jump in the shower again with the desperate urge to scrub away what I have just done. Hopping out, I dry off and slip my silk black dressing gown on. I make my way through all the dresses in my wardrobe until I find one that catches my eye and will be perfect for tonight.

A short tight bright pink dress with no sleeves. The dress is stunning. Although it has no sleeves it has black lace on the bottom half of the skirt. Before I put the dress on, I catch a glance of the clock, and I see I still have an hour to get ready. I stay in my silk gown and go to my makeup table.

Deciding on going slightly gothic, I put light eyeliner and dark pink eyeshadow on, adding mascara to make my eyelashes look longer and thicker. I go simple with the blush and choose light pink lipstick. I tie my hair up in a bun and curl my bangs on either side of my fringe. The clock flashes, 6:30. I stand up and pull my shoe boxes out of the bottom of my wardrobe and choose my black boot heels.

I open the duffle bag on my bed and stare at the contents in amazement. I only have ten minutes before Jemma arrives, but there's so much stuff to use. Evil things and ways to kill swarmed through my head. This task was going to drive me crazy and insane. I reach in and pull out a knife that has a thigh strap attached to it and wrap it around my thigh. I reach in and pull a smaller one in a protective cover and slip it between my breasts.

I zip up the bag and stuff it under my bed just as Jemma toots the car horn outside my house. I sprint downstairs and head for the door. I plop myself down in the passenger seat of her car.
"Hey," she greets me with excitement. Her face is shiny with a massive ear to ear smile.
"Let's go," I smile back at her.

We arrive at Fishnets bar looking sexy as hell. Walking

up to the bouncer, skipping the long line, I give him a flirty smile then whisper the code word in his ear that Martin has given me. He lets us in straight away. The look on Jemma's face gives away how surprised she is.

"Wow," she exclaims.

"Yeah, I know," I giggle

She pulls me over to the bar and orders us both cocktails. Sour Sue for her and a Bloody Mary for me. We drink our drinks as I spot Lucas walk in.

"Hey, I'm going to dance," I say, swinging off my bar stool.

"Okay I'll go see how many guys I can flirt with," she responded. It was a game we both liked to play.

"Meet back here," I call over my shoulder to her as I go to find Lucas.

Crossing the dance floor to get to Lucas, guys keep coming up behind me trying to grind against me. After a few get their feet stomped on by me, they got the point. I eventually see Lucas standing in a corner with a girl. I make my way over to them. Just as I am almost in front of them, Lucas looks up and sees me. He smiles at me, not knowing what's about to come. I walk right up to them and smile in a flirty manner.

"Hey Lucas," I purr seductively. The girl he has with him looks at me with disgust before huffing and walking away.

"Thanks Monster, I've been trying to get rid of her for ages," Lucas smiles, giving me a one-armed hug.

"That's okay," I grin. "Want to dance and get some drinks?" I ask.
"My Shout," he says happily.

We go over to the bar and order a dirty Martini for him and a Bourbon for me. Sculling back our drinks, we make our way onto the dance floor. Slowly we started to grind against each other. After a while Lucas's hand starts roaming over my body, thankfully missing what I have concealed away. I decide that now would be a good time to complete the 'task'.

"Let's go somewhere more private," Lucas seductively purrs in my ear. Quickly I nod, pulling him behind me towards a room at the back of the club. Lucas pulls open the door and gestures for me to enter. I enter slowly and see that the room we are in looks like a semi hidden BDSM room, currently empty other than the bed in the middle of the room. I pull Lucas towards the middle of the room swaying my hips seductively.

What I'm about to do is going to be very bad but also a lot of fun. I move his hands from his sides and place them on my hips. He pulls me close to him and starts to kiss down my neck, stopping occasionally to suck on a soft spot. I wrap my arms around his neck and bring my knee up, connecting with his nuts. He collapses to the floor holding his hands over his nuts, protectively in pain. I mentally chuckle. I've always wanted to do that. At least it would look like he was sexually assaulting a girl before he was found.

Mollie's POV

I reach up my dress and unhook the knife from its thigh strap. I slowly spin it in my hand. How was I going to do this? I move so he is underneath me and I am straddling him. Pinning his arms to his sides with my knees. I bring the knife up with two hands and plunge it through his heart.

Jumping back quickly to stop blood getting on me. Straightening my dress, I exit the room and go to find Jemma. Looking around I find Jemma flirting with a guy at the bar. A thought passes through my mind 'Where did I put the knife?!'. Then I remember I put it back in its safety strap, under my dress.

"Hey Jemma," I say smiling once I've caught her attention.
"Monster, I would like you to meet this lovely hulk James. He's a year older than us." she purrs happily.
"Hello," the man sitting with her says to me, trying to be polite but I can tell he is angry at me for interrupting.
"What do you want?" He tries not to bellow at me.
I shiver slightly, not liking his tone. It holds dominance and control. Two things I don't like a man to have.

"Jemma," I direct my words to her. Ignoring what 'Mr. I have Control' has to say.
"I'm going home, do you want to come with me, or do you want to stay with him?" I ask, jerking my thumb towards James.

"I'm going to stay. But you can take my car if you like. You seem more sober than me," she offers.
"Okay, thanks Jemma. Text me when you get home. Okay?"
"Okay," she replies, giving me her keys.
"Love you, talk later," I give her a kiss and leave.

Lucas' death isn't weighing on my mind like I thought it would. I didn't think I would be able to do it. I make my way towards Jemma's car, taking long strides. Opening the car door, I look around before hopping in. The lack of people searching for a killer or police coming to see the body shocks me. It was like no one noticed me with him.

I arrive back at home and park Jemma's car on the side of the house. I reach the front door and twist the handle. Shit, it's unlocked. When I left, I knew I locked it. This only means one thing. Some dangerous asshole is in my house waiting for me. I pull the knife out of its thigh strap for the second time tonight. I slowly open the door just enough to slip my hand in and turn on the lights. I open it a bit wider and enter the house, closing and locking the door behind me.

I slowly make my way into the kitchen and find no one, so I continue my investigation around the house. I stop walking when I see the lounge light on. 'I don't remember turning that on,' I think to myself.
Slowly I make my way towards the lounge. I peek around the corner and don't believe what I see.

"Drew!" I yell at the boy sitting on my couch, reading a book. "WHAT THE HELL DO YOU THINK YOU'RE DOING IN MY HOUSE!?"

"I had to make sure you did it one way or another, didn't I sweetie?" he says casually turning a page.

"WELL, I DID, NOW GET OUT OF MY HOUSE!" I yell at him.

He snaps the book shut before getting up off the couch and casually strolling over to me. He kisses me on the forehead before saying "Okay my little Monster. Your first pay is on your bed along with Task Two," I stay rooted to the floor as he waltzes out of my house, calling a goodbye as he leaves.

"Finally!" I breathe out, happier now that he has gone. I slowly make my way to my room. Opening my door, I spy another manilla folder and wads of cash on my bed. I rush from my doorway to my bed and collapse on t, holding the cash in my hands. Oh, The things people will do for money.

Laughing at myself I pick up all the cash and put it in the weapon bag. I walk back over to my bed and pull my PJs out from under my pillow and head to the bathroom. Stripping off, I hop into a newly run bath filled with bubbles that fill the air with a sweet scent of vanilla. I let the water swallow me whole. It feels good; staying in the water until it turns cold, and the vanilla scent had soaked into my skin. After what felt like hours, I get out and flop into my bed. I spend the night tossing and turning, afraid that Drew is going to hurt my family.

My mother rushes into my room, ripping open the curtains and pulling my covers off me. She may be my mother, but I sure do hate her sometimes. It's times like this, I want my own place.
"What do you want, mother?" I groan sleepily, pulling my covers back over me.
"Get your lazy ass out of bed and get downstairs, your boyfriend is waiting for you. He said he was taking you out today," she pulls the covers off me again.

"Tell him to go away, I'm sleeping," I groan, pulling my covers on me again. "Wait, why are you home now?" I ask, remembering she said she was going to be spending the night at her friend's house.
"Mollie it's 4 in the bloody afternoon!" she snaps at me as she stomps out of my bedroom. I drag myself out of bed, making my way to the bathroom. I stop halfway and look at my desk.

The manilla folder is still there. Curiosity about the next task gets the best of me. I walk over and sit down at my desk, opening the folder. I start reading who is next… Declan. I read the information given:

Name: Declan Kennedy
Common Hangout: Luda Arcade
Location: 3/4 Luda Plains
Deadline: Tuesday

The arcade is always empty. Why would he hang out there? A knock on the door drags me out of my thoughts, quickly I shove the papers back into the dirty manilla folder and hide it in my desk. "Come in," I call out. Zaid opens the door and comes in. Thank God I put my silk gown on otherwise he would have seen my birthday suit.

"You're still not ready!" he exclaims, stomping his feet like a little child who hasn't gotten his own way.

"You look funny doing that," I say, getting up and walking over to him. I wrap my arms around his neck.

He pulls me close against him, so close that I can feel the outline of his abs against my front.

"Let me get dressed then you can take me out for breakfast," I say softly, planting a kiss on his cheek.

"Babe you know it's 4 in the afternoon right?" he chuckles. The stupid boy laughs at me, how dare he!

"Shut up. If I want pancakes and bacon at four in the bloody afternoon, I'll have them at four in the bloody afternoon," I snap at him, pushing him out of my room.

I stroll into the lounge. Looking out the window I can see that it's a hot day. Thank goodness I decided to wear skinny jeans and an old wife beater. I find Zaid sitting on the couch talking with my mother, I decide I want you to have a little fun.

"RAT!" I shriek, jumping up off the ground, waving my arms in the air and pointing at a random place in the room.

You Make Me Crazy

My mother jumps up on the couch screaming, clutching to Zaid with a horrified look on her ageing face. I stop jumping and pointing and just stare at my mother before starting to laugh.

"Oh, mom you really fell for it," I cackle, doubling over.

"There's no rat?" she asks suspiciously.

"No. ma'am there's no rat," Zaid says, trying to stay straight-faced, while untangling my mother from him.

"Oh, well I'm sorry," mother untangles herself and sits properly on the couch next to him.

"So…" I start "Where are we going for our date?"

"It's a surprise," Zaid responses, getting up quickly. "We should be leaving now," he continues, pulling me towards the door.

"Mother," I turn to her, "Did you say this was okay?" I struggle against Zaid's grip.

"Yes I did darling. Now go!" She shoos me towards the door.

When we arrive at Luda Arcade. I panic quickly, wondering if Zaid knows something or if he somehow managed to read the file hidden in my desk.

"Why are we here?" I ask slightly worried.

"I want to show you our favourite gaming zone, and where we're meeting Declan for the comp," he answers, wrapping his arm around my waist.

"Oh… Okay let's go then?" I found myself asking it more as a question.

I'm surprised by what I see when we get inside.

Mollie's POV

Everywhere I look, I see gaming consoles. This is like the gambling zone at a casino but for youngsters. "Wow!" I exclaim loudly. I hear Zaid chuckling next to me.

"Come on, I can see Declan over at his favourite shooting game," he pulls me over to a game that has two fake guns with long cords. One pink and one teal. "Hey Z," Declan smiles, doing a weird handshake with Zaid. "Hey M," he pulls me into a quick hug and gives me a quick peck on the cheek.

"Hey to you, Declan," I laugh seeing Zaid's face when Declan kisses my cheek. "Aww Zaid lighten up I'm with you, don't you remember?" I giggle.

"Fine whatever," he huffs. "Let's play. Declan and I first."

I stand beside them, watching them play. They are so into the game; they are practically ignoring me. I decide I'm going to look around to learn more about this place for the task. I walk around, marvelling at how big the space is. I look around slowly studying the area. I locate a hidden door near a few games, just out of view. I walk over and find the door is unlocked. I reach for the handle and pull it open.

Before I walk through, I look around me, to see if anyone is watching me. No one seems to be watching, so I walk in and turn on the lights. Inside the room I saw a gaming machine just like the one the boys are currently playing. Above the game sits a sign that reads

You Make Me Crazy

'Final Play Off, Winner Takes All'. I know now exactly how I am going to annihilate Declan.

I exit the room and close the door behind me, walking back over to the boys. To my surprise, they are exactly where I left them.

"Hey guys I'm back, did you miss me?" I tease, wrapping my arms around Zaid.

"Oh hey babe, did you go somewhere?" he asks, not pulling his eyes away from the game.

"Oh my gosh, Zaid you haven't been paying me any attention at all! I feel so hurt!" I fake feeling hurt by putting my hand over my heart.

"Oh I'm really sorry baby," he apologizes.

"I'm going home. I'm tired and bored here." I turn around and walk out of Luda Arcade. I walk all the way home, it takes me ages to get back. I almost cried over the fact that Zaid didn't come after me. Did he ever care? I get to the front door and my mother opens it before I can even grab the door knob.

She must sense that something is wrong because as soon as she sees me, she pulls me into her arms. I break out into ugly sobs before she can ask me anything.

"Are you okay Mollie?" she asks once I've calmed down. I move to sit on the couch.

"He took me out and just ignored me and when I left, he didn't come after me," I sob into the pillow I've just picked up off the couch.

Mollie's POV

"Hey darling it's okay, he's just acting like a guy," my mother tries to console me.

"I know, but I think I really like him," I began to cry again.

"It will be okay, just go to bed and have a sleep in. I'll wake you up at noon tomorrow for pancakes," My mother pulls me up off the couch and pushes me towards my bedroom.

"Okay, goodnight mother," I say, dragging myself to my room. I get into bed, fully clothed after taking my shoes off. Once my head hits the pillow, I let sleep consume me.

Zaid's POV

I watched her walk off leaving Declan and I in the arcade. She looked sad and hurt. I can't believe I was such an idiot that I got so wrapped up into the game that I ignored her. Saying I didn't know she walked off the first time would be a lie... I noticed. I couldn't feel her around me, and I felt sad that she had just walked off while Declan and I were playing.

"Hey man, are you okay? You look lost in thought," Declan asks bringing me out of my thoughts
"I think I should go after her," I start getting ready to leave.
"Zaid, just leave her, you don't need to follow her everywhere. You need to remember that she's a girl, and they get moody at times," he says, pulling me back towards him and the game.
"Fine. One more game then I'm leaving," I huff.

Some Time Later

"Yes," Declan yells after winning the game.
"Okay, I'm going now, I have homework to do, that's due in tomorrow," I lie. Tomorrow I am going to get Mollie to talk to me, I need to know if she's okay.
"See ya man," Declan calls, as he starts another game. This arcade will be the death of him one day.

Zaid's POV

Walking out of the arcade, I pull out my phone and dial Mollie's number. It goes to her voicemail. Why isn't she answering? I look at the time on my phone. It's just gone ten pm, she can't be asleep yet, it's too early. I call her five more times, but she still doesn't answer. I didn't realise she was so upset that she would ignore me. I give in and send her a text instead:

```
Baby I'm sorry, I didn't mean to upset
you.
I'm sorry I didn't pay attention. If
you're
okay, I'll pick you up tomorrow, and take
you on a proper date.
I Love You XX
- Zaid
```

I really hope she replies and agrees to go out with me on that date. Slowly, I drive home, back to my place; as I mentally plan the perfect date for my beautiful Monster.

Mollie's POV

M ollie," I hear my mother whisper in my ear. I groan and roll over.

"Come on honey, pancakes are on the table waiting for you," she says sweetly.

"Fine," I mumble. I know it's lunch time already, and that I've slept for 14 hours, but I don't really care.

Slowly I get up and walk, half asleep, down to the kitchen, where I am greeted by the intoxicating smell of blueberry pancakes with chocolate. I sit down at the table after grabbing my phone from where my mother left it to charge. I cut my pancakes into smaller pieces and opened my phone. I see I have six missed calls from Zaid and a text message from him as well. I read the message then decide that I don't want to see him today, but I still have to get the task done. So, I reply:

```
I'll meet you at Fishface Eatery at 2pm.
See you then.
```

I finish my pancakes and do my dishes, like a good girl. Still with my phone in my pocket, I decide that I will try to see if Declan is at Luda Arcade today.

```
What's up its Monster.
Are you going to Luda Arcade today?
I heard there was a comp on and
```

Mollie's POV

I wanted to wish you luck.

I am about to go back to my room to have a luxurious shower and get dressed. When I receive two text messages.

From Declan:
Yeah, I'm competing
today babe, thanks for
wanting to say good luck
If you want to see me after
come down at 2:20pm to see
me win the final.

I send back a quick 'Okay, I'll see you then' and then I read Zaid's text:

From Zaid:
I'm truly sorry. I will
make it up to you when
I see you. Love you X

I'm not going to reply because if I did, I know I would say something I will end up regretting. Rushing to my room I get ready. Jumping into the shower cleaning myself off, I get dressed in my tight red skinny jeans and black studded top. Pulling on my knee boots I grab the bag out from under my bed. Opening it up I began to think of how I will get it done.

41

Unzipping it, I pull out a wire cord, before closing the bag back up; I stand up and walk to my wardrobe and get my Vans bag. After putting the wire into the bag, I grab my phone, keys and wallet. Checking my phone, I see that it is ten minutes to 2 o'clock. I run out of the house, locking the door behind me.

Twenty minutes later, I arrive at the arcade. Looking around I spot Declan standing at the game he and Zaid were playing yesterday. Near him is a charge with each computer and their ranking. Declan is at the top of the rank winning every game.
"Now for the final round to determine the champion," I hear a voice announce over the intercom. "Would Declan Kennedy, champ 3 years running, and Ryan the champ from 4 years ago please come to the finals zone?"
Everyone shuffles into the small room I had found yesterday. Standing near the entrance I see Declan approach me.

"Hey Monster," he says flirtatiously
"Good luck, I hear you made it through to the finals," I congratulate him. He puts his arm around my shoulder and pulls me along with him to the final room. "Go in and win. I'll wait out here, the room is too small," I remove his arm from my shoulder, just as I receive a text.

From Zaid:

Mollie's POV

```
You stood me up Monster,
I thought you wanted to be
with me.
```

My body fills with guilt, as I start to feel terrible.

```
Zaid, I am so sorry something came up.
I forgot to tell you.
Meet me at my place at 7. I'll
cook you some dinner.
Love you XX
```

I hope this task doesn't take much more of my time.

"Sorry that was Zaid," I apologize to Declan.
"That's okay, wasn't he meant to take you out on a date?" he asks, pulling me by the hand into the room.
"I cancelled on him coming here," I admit following him.
"Aww you did that for me? Oh, that's sweet," he exclaims, kissing me on the cheek.

I laugh at his childish ways. "Go win and I'll give you a surprise afterwards."
"Stay here," he commands at me running over to the game.
Minutes later I hear the theme song at the beginning of the game.
"On your mark, get set, SHOOT!" the voice on the intercom calls.

You Make Me Crazy

Loud gunshot noises fill the room as everyone starts shouting encouraging words at Declan and Ryan. Only minutes later the crowd erupts in a roar as Declan wins. He walks over to me and picks me up by the waist and twirling me around.

"Congrats," I giggle as he put me down kissing my cheek.
"It was worth coming then, wasn't it?" he asks, laughing at me stumbling a bit from my dizziness.
"Yup," I giggle, grabbing onto his hand, he has held out for me.

Bringing me close in his arms I look around and notice that everyone has left leaving the two of us alone in the room together. Declan brings me to his chest wrapping his arms tightly around me. I bring my arms up around his neck, my bag resting on my wrist. Slowly he leans forward and softly begins kissing me. I lean into the kiss while slowly unzipping my bag, trying to make sure he doesn't hear anything. When I manage to get the wire into my hand, I drop the bag as quietly as possible. Declan pulls me even closer, taking over my lips with his, dominating the kiss.

I pull back, bringing my arms with me wrapping the rope around his neck. With the speed of light and without him noticing at first, I lean back quickly, choking him. Falling back, I fall flat on my butt, pulling Declan down on top of me, dead.

As fast as possible I push him off me and jump into action. I move the body behind the game. Dusting myself off I put everything back into the bag, careful not to leave anything behind. I pull my phone out to check the time. It's almost four in the evening and I still have to cook Zaid dinner.

I leave the room making sure that the coast is clear I find the entire room is empty and there are no cameras to be seen. Running to the door, I rush all the way home, and up the stairs into my bedroom. I rip the bag of weapons out from under my bed and stashed the rope into it. Feeling dirty after having that dead body on top of me, I need to have a shower to make myself feel better.

Half an hour later I emerge squeaky clean. Walking out of my bathroom, stepping into my bedroom, I notice the French doors are open. The curtains swaying with the invisible breeze. On my bed lay a manilla file. Drew must have been here. I walk towards my bed being cautious that he may still be in the room. I move qu ckly to the bed grabbing the folder off it. As I pick it up, a piece of paper flutters out of it. With my empty hand, I pick it up. It reads:

Great job on completing the task.
Here is your next task. Do it

well. Also, nice singing, in the
shower.

- Drew XX

"That bastard," I scoff. How dare he break into my room just to give me the next task! I am fuming. He's going to get it. In a rush I get dressed and grab the files. I sit at my pale faded desk. As I open the file, my only hope is that it isn't Zaid.

The file reads:

```
Name: Troy Thompson
Hangout: Scarline Race Track
Location: Just off the motorway exit 7014
Deadline: Wednesday
```

There's a race Tuesday night, not believing that the next 'target' is my best friend's boyfriend, I walk downstairs. I can't hurt Jemma like that! I cannot kill Troy. It's just something I can't do.

Whilst having a mental argument with myself, I start to get the food prepared, for dinner with Zaid. Knowing my mother won't be home until tomorrow. I begin to make my favourite burgers, I only make these when my mother isn't home, she hates the taste and smell of them.

I made the patties and while they sit for half an hour in

the fridge, I start to grate the carrot and cheese. I still have to slice the tomato, beetroot, lettuce, pickles and my brother's favourite ingredient, pineapple. I only make these when Anthony comes home, to stay.

A knock on the door pulls me from my thoughts about Anthony. Walking over to it I look at my phone and see that it's only 6:30pm.
"Hey," Zaid greets me as I open the door.
"Hey," I reply back awkwardly. I really hope tonight isn't going to be as awkward as I think it will be. "Come in."

We walk into the kitchen and he finds a seat at the bar table while I begin to fry the patties.
"I'm sorry, I didn't meet you earlier today," I say sadly, not looking at him since I feel so guilty.
"It's okay, I'm sorry for ignoring you while we're at the arcade yesterday, so I guess we're even," he says, trying to make it sound okay.
"Yeah I guess," I say flipping the patties, seeing as they are perfectly cooked, I put them on a plate and say "Come on, dinner's ready,"

We sit down and start making our burgers. We sit in silence, just as we are about to eat my phone rings. I get up from the table as I say, "Excuse me, sorry Zaid," as I answer my phone.
"Hello Mollie speaking."
"Hey little sis."
"OMG Anthony!" I exclaim.
"Yeah it's me little sis. I guess you missed me?" he

teases.

"Yes, of course I miss you, you idiot. I love you so much!" I look over to Zaid and find his face lowered, he looks really sad and hurt.

"Well you can tell me all about what's up, when I come home in two weeks."

"Yay! I can't wait, I'm so excited. Sorry I have to go, I'm having dinner with my boyfriend, Zaid."

"Okay see you soon. Love you lots Monster."

"Love you too Anthony," I hang up and sat back down.

"I'm sorry about that, Zaid, I didn't know he was going to call."

"No, it's fine. Your ex-boyfriend is coming back, and you still love him. It's fine. I'll go," he says, getting up walking towards the door. This brings tears to my eyes, and I start to cry.

"Why are you crying?" he snaps at me. "You still love your ex-boyfriend, yet you still go out with me."

I sob for a while when I realise that he thinks Anthony is my ex-boyfriend.

"You're my first boyfriend," I sob.

"Yeah right, if I am then who is Anthony?" he is angry, very angry.

Still sobbing I reply, feeling hurt, "He's my brother."

"What the… oh shit. I'm sorry Mollie. I didn't mean to get angry, I just didn't know," he comes over and wraps his arms around me trying to comfort me. "Come on, let's finish eating. I have something I want to tell you after."

Mollie's POV

In silence, we finish eating dinner. What would normally taste delicious to me tastes foul and horrible because I feel sick with hurt and pain from what Zaid has said Offering to help do the dishes, Zaid and I clear the table. Not long after, we are sitting in the lounge.

"So what do you want to talk about?" I ask him, sitting awkwardly on one side of the three-seater couch.

"You… we shouldn't keep having to be this awkward, you know what I mean right?"

"Yeah I know, it's just, well you jumped to conclusions; guessing my brother was my ex-boyfriend."

"You never told me about your family."

"True, well there is my mother, Grace. My older brother, Anthony and sister, Silvia. My father is dead. Other than that, there is my cousin, you know her, Heather."

"I'm sorry."

"Okay, it's late, I should get going."

"Oh okay. I'll see you at school tomorrow?"

"I'll come by and pick you up in the morning." he kisses me on the lips bringing me into a hug. "I love you."

"See you then."

The next day goes fast, no one seems to notice that Lucas and Declan are missing. That must have been how Drew Martin wanted it. All day I receive evil looks from Drew. It reminds me that if I don't do what he wants my family's lives are on the line.

"Jemma!" I yell running at her, pulling her into a tight hug.

49

"Haha, what's up Monster?" she pulls me into her, hugging me back twice as tightly.
"Guess what!"
"What!" she questions knowing that it would be good news.
"Anthony's coming home!" I yell happily.
"OMG when?" Jemma yells back. At one point she had a crush on my brother, but then again who wouldn't? He had the body of a god. If he wasn't my brother I would tap that.

"In two weeks, he said. I can't wait to see him, I hope he brings me another Letterman Jacket of his," I love his jackets.
"Are we gonna have a burger night like last time he came? We could invite all the boys," she suggests just as Drew, Zaid, Troy and James walk up to us.
"What's this about burger night?" James asks, licking his lips.
"Yeah because count me in," Troy says looking hopeful.
"Anthony is coming home, and every time he does Jemma and I throw him a burger night," I say knowing that Drew will do something to stop this.

"And who is Anthony?" Drew asks, smirking. I could already see what he was thinking.
"My brother, so unless you're gay, you high baboon, don't think about trying anything," calling him a baboon ticked him off.
"Your brother is gay?!" Zaid questions.
Jemma and I crack up laughing. We laugh until there

are tears in our eyes and we are both bent over clutching our sides.

"Wow you are an idiot," Jemma says sobering up. "My brother isn't gay, the looks on your faces are priceless. Anthony's girlfriend died a few years ago."
"Oh," all the guys say
"And also my niece," tears started rolling down my cheeks. Just thinking about it is too painful.

"Calais and my niece Latisha were at the park; three hooded guys came up to them and drugged them with chloroform. Calais and Latisha were taken away to a place not far from Luda Arcade, where they were kept in a basement. Latisha was only eight years old, she was savagely beaten black and blue, then raped for the last three days of her life. Calais watched all this happen for over a week. Once police found them, the kidnappers had escaped and there were only the bodies left. Anthony, my mother and I cried for weeks after that, we happen to be the only family Calais has left."

There is a stream of tears running down my cheeks. Zaid wraps his arms tightly around me, while I cry into his shoulder. Jemma pulls me away from him and into her arms.
"Hey, calm down M," she says soothingly. "Do you want me to take you home?"
"Yes please," I say in between sobs. I'm not in a state of mind to do anything.
"I'm taking her home. Stay away, you got it?" she warns

the boys.
"Yes," they say at the same time.

Tiredly Jemma helps me walk into my bedroom.
Carefully she lays me down on my bed and lays down
with me.
"You okay Monster?"
"Nah not really Jemma."
"Should I go make you some pancakes?"
"You sure you're okay with that?"
"Yeah, I'll be back with them shortly okay?" She gets up
off my bed and walks down to the kitchen.

Just as I roll over I receive a text message.
From Zaid:

```
Hey babe hope you're
okay. Tomorrow night
I'm taking you to Scarline
Race Tracks. Troy is
racing but doesn't want
Jemma to watch yet. I'll
pick you up @ 4pm
Love you XX
```

I bet Drew has something to do with this.

I sent back a reply, 'Yes, see you then' just as I
hear Jemma curse loudly.
"You motherfucking stove!" she screams. My guess is

that she has burnt herself. I get up off my bed and walk into the kitchen to see if she's okay.

Walking past the mirror in the hallway, I see that I have tear stains running down my face like a dried-up waterfall, smudged mascara and eyeliner doesn't help the look either, nor does my messy bird nest from lying on my bed. "Jemma you okay?" I ask, walking into the kitchen. She has her hand under the tap, with cold water running over it.
"Your mother's stupid stove did it again," she mutters.
"You sure it's not the person working it?" I tease.
"NO!" she shouts while laughing.
"Come on, I'll help you finish them, then I'll go to sleep; all that crying took it out of me, I'm tired."

Walking up to my bedroom, I feel full. I must remember to never eat Jemma's pancakes again, she puts too many toppings on them. Flopping down on my bed   fall asleep instantly.

Stretching, I wake up, 'Shit!' I panic as I look at the time. It's past lunch time and a school day. Struggling I pull myself out of bed and to my desk to check my phone. I have three unread messages. One from Zaid, Mother and Drew.

From Zaid:

```
Hope you're feeling okay
for tonight, seeing as
```

```
you're not at school today.
See you @ 4pm.
```

From Drew:

```
Have fun tonight.
Don't forget that
the deadline is
Tomorrow.
```

From Mother:

```
Morning darling, Jemma told
me about what happened
yesterday so I called up
and said you would be off
today. Talk to you tonight
if I see you before I go out.
```

Just as I reply 'Thank you' to my mum I get another text from Zaid, saying that he will pick me up in two hours. Quickly I grab a banana and go to have a shower. Getting out of the shower I walk over to my closet pulling out my sparkly black skinny jeans and a white top.

I sit down on my bed and pull out my laptop. Plugging in my headphones I blast American Idiot by Green Day. I open up my emails, as I sing along, and see an email from an unknown email address and sender.

Mollie's POV

```
MONSTER!
IF YOU CAN'T COMPLETE YOUR TASK,
YOUR MOTHER, SISTER, BEST FRIEND AND
NOW YOUR BROTHER WILL GET IT!
AFTER THEY ARE GONE, IT WILL
BE ON YOUR COUSINS SHOULDERS.
```

That shitface Martin! I'm going to get him back for this. How dare he threaten my family, and especially my sister - who he hasn't even met - and Jemma, my best friend. Just as I was about to reply I got a Skype call from my sister, Sylvia.

"Hey Sylvia," I answer, trying to sound happy.
"Hey sis, long time no talk!"
"Yeah I know, sorry. I got a new boyfriend, who I've been busy with".
"Ahhh!" she screams. "My little sister got her first boyfriend and didn't tell me! I'm not that old to not be excited."
"Sorry. I think I might have told Anthony when he called up the other day."
"ANTHONY KNEW BEFORE ME! YOU TOLD YOUR 30-YEAR-OLD BROTHER BEFORE YOUR 25-YEAR-OLD SISTER!" she yells at me.
"He's from a band…"

"WAIT WHAT!? YOU'RE DATING A GUY FROM A BAND! WHAT BAND? IS HE FAMOUS?"
"Yes, and from Four Singers and a Casket."

She screams so loud that it hurts my eardrums.
"SHUT UP SYLVIA!" I yell at her. "Oh, and Jemma's
going out with Troy."
"That lucky bitch!!" she replies.
I crack up laughing before she continues, "So little
sister, who's the famous guy allowed to kiss your lips?"
"Zaid," I mumble.
"Zaid as in Zaid Yousuf!?"
This is why I never talk to my family about my love life.
"Yes sis. Sorry I have to go; he will be here soon to pick
me up and go to Scarline Race Track"
"Oh well okay. Say hello to mum for me and tell her I will
be home in a few months. And don't do anything with
Zaid that I wouldn't do"
"OMG Sylvia! That's everything and also the same thing
Jemma said"
"Have fun baby sis. Talk soon"
"Bye!"

I log off my laptop and shut it down. Far out! She can
talk for a long time. I have twenty minutes to get ready
before Zaid arrives. Getting up off my bed my phone
dings letting me know I had a notification. Opening my
phone, I let out a breath I didn't know I was holding, it is
just a text from my brother, Anthony.

From Bro-Bro:

Hey baby sis, I just got a
text from Sylvia about your

```
date. Don't do anything I
will need to beat him up for.
Have fun. I love you lots
baby sister xx
```

I let out a long laugh. Oh, there is my brother's protective side.

To Bro-Bro:

```
Chill bro and thanks, but
there will be no beating up.
Love you lots xx
```

I walk into my bathroom and look in the mirror. Through all that has been happening, I look better than ever. Smiling at myself, I pick up my toothpaste and toothbrush and start to brush my teeth. Spitting out my toothpaste, I grab my make-up kit and start on a semi natural/semi mysterious look.

After finishing I skip happily into my bedroom to put on my combat boots and white leather jacket and collect my phone, wallet, shoulder bag, lip gloss and pull out the nun-chucks from the bag under my bed. I hear the doorbell ring and ran down the stairs. I pull the door open.

Standing at the door dressed in jeans and a tight white shirt with a black leather jacket, looking casual but not as hell is Zaid.

"Hey babe. Are you ready to go?" he greets me with a smile.

"Yes I am ready. I just have to, look up" I say, pecking his cheek and grabbing my keys.

We walked out the door locking it after us, and head to his car. Just as I sat down in the passenger seat I remember when he first drove me somewhere on his bike.

"Zaid, what happened to your bike?" I ask him.

"When the guys and I arrived here, we brought a few cars to use. This is James' and mine"

"Oh that's cool. I wish I had one this flash" I comment.

"This isn't flash, you haven't seen our limo yet" he laughs at me.

"Show off!" I chide him. "Come on just drive me to the races"

We pull into the car park with the gravel flying everywhere. Bringing the car to a stop, Zaid get out and opens my door. I get out and thank him, taking hold of his arm. Almost running we head towards where the drivers are, I notice Troy gearing up.

"Hey Troy!" Zaid yells at him, making him turn his head towards us.

"Monster! Zaid!" he yells back at us.

Together we walk over to him. My eyes widened as round as saucers; I was shocked! I never knew Troy was a racer, I'm sure Jemma doesn't know as well. Stupid boys, stupid secrets.

Mollie's POV

"By the look on your face Mollie, I am guessing your boy-toy here didn't tell you I was a racer" Troy chuckles.
"Hey! I am not a boy-toy!" Zaid exclaims, sounding offended.
"Chill man! He was joking" I laugh at Zaid. "And no Troy, Dumbo here didn't tell me"
"Shame! Your girl called you a Dumbo!" Troy points at Zaid.
"Hmph" Zaid stomps, acting like a little kid who hasn't gotten his own way. Damn! This guy loves acting like a little kid.
"Monster, you might want to take your 'little kid' here and go sit in the stands. Meet me back here afterwards without the 'kid' and I'll show you the ropes" Troy says before pulling on his helmet.
"Come on Zaid. See you soon Troy and good luck" I tug Zaid by the arm towards the stands. We take our seats next to each other right at the top so we can have a better view.

"ON YOUR MARKS" a voice booms over the speakers.
"BRRR" a loud buzzer sounded…and then they're off.
"Thompson coming first, Rose coming second. Oh no! Wait Newton's coming close to first place! Neck and neck Thompson and Newton, who's going to win?"
The crowd is going absolutely wild.

"Newton first, Thompson second and Rose third, leaving everyone else still racing!"
I look over at Zaid only to see that he has fallen asleep.

You Make Me Crazy

This is my chance. Jumping up I run down to Troy leaving Zaid sleeping in the stands.

"Monster" Troy calls out to me as he sees me running over.

"Hey! How about we go into our own private place?" I ask seductively.

"Let's go!" he grabs my arm pulling me into a little room, closed off and hidden away from everyone, locking the door behind us.

He pushes me up against the door.

"w-what are you doing Troy?" I stutter.

"Giving you a private lesson on cars" he plants a slobbery kiss on my lips.

I don't like it. Slowly, I slip my hand into my bag and grab my nunchucks. Just as I am about to pull them out I bite down on his lower lip piercing it, making it bleed. He jumps back from me, and I swing the nun chucks hitting him across the face.

"Ouch" he yelps out. I don't stop there, swinging at him again and again. I get him down on the floor clutching pieces of his body. With one last swing across the head, I manage to knock him out, to make sure I have finished the task I get down and straddle his body. Placing my hands tightly around his throat, I begin to squeeze his throat until I am sure he is dead. Getting my nunchucks I stand up and remove any evidence that I have been here.

Walking out of the stands I see that Zaid is looking for

me. He has his back turned so I race up and jump on his back, surprising him.

"Whoa!" he exclaims, holding me tight making me giggle. "Are you ready to go?"

"Yup I'm ready. I went and said goodbye to Troy while you were asleep so we can just go." I say holding on tightly while he piggy backs me to his car.

The car pulls into my driveway and Zaid gets out to open my door for me. Slipping my legs out I stand up and take his hand pulling him into the house, tugging him into my room and we collapse on my bed.

"Isn't your mum going to be home soon?" he asks, tightening his arms around my waist. "I should go before she gets here."

"Its fine, she isn't coming home tonight. She is working a late shift, so she is staying at a 'workmates'" I say snuggling into him.

"Okay" he mumbles into my hair wrapping his arm tightly around me slowly he trails kisses down my neck to my collar bone.

"Mmm" I moan "Zaid, what are you doing?" feeling nothing but pleasure and pure bliss.

"Just going to give you the best time of your life" he says before rolling on top of me holding all his weight off me.

"Is that okay with you princess?" he teasingly kisses my forehead, nose, cheeks and lips.

"You seem so sure that it will be the best time of my life" I stick my tongue out at him.

61

You Make Me Crazy

"Oh, should I prove to you that it will be?"
"You can try," I tease, knowing I won't regret it.
"Okay baby, I promise you won't regret it" he says as he quickly strips all our clothes off.

He brings his lips down lightly kissing my lips, slowly licking my bottom lips asking for entrance which I grant him without a second thought. This kiss is passionate and full of love, I couldn't ask for anything more. His hands sliding down my body sends shivers down my spine, his hands come down to my butt squeezing it lightly and making me gasp. This boy is full of surprises, and he has made me wet, wetter than I have ever been before. I feel his lips on my neck near my collar and his hand on my clit slowly rubbing it.

When I relax enough he slips one finger in, and I tighten from the intrusion. Slowly he starts making a 'come here' action with his finger, butterflies and the feeling of pleasure swarm my stomach. Without realising it I let out a moan. After hearing that he slips in another finger and starts to pump them in and out,

"Oh shit" I call out "I'm so close". I feel his hard on pressed up against the inside of the thigh. Quickly, he removes his fingers and lines up his tip with my hole. Pleasure choruses through my body as he slips his length in slowly. After a moment or two of letting me get used to him, he pulls out slightly then pushes back in slowly, slowly going getting faster and faster with each thrust.

Mollie's POV

He keeps going and I keep letting out moans until we both each have our own release at the same time. I milk him tightly, his seed filling every inch of me, it was only now that I realise he has fucked me raw, but I don't care. Zaid pulls out and lays down next to me pulling me into his arms, I don't care at all that we are both still naked.

"So baby, was that the best time of your life?" Zaid asks, kissing my lips deeply after asking.

"Yes, it was Zaidy-Po," I giggle like the little school girl I am.

"Ready to go again then?" he passionately starts kissing my lips again rolling over on top of me.

I wake up in a startled fright as I hear my alarm going off on my bedside table. Rolling over, I find I am restricted due to a big strong arm that is wrapped tightly around my waist. As I try to sit up, pain shoots through my body as I remember the four rounds we had that ended early in the morning.

"Zaid" I whisper in his ear hoping to wake him up.

"Morning baby" his deep morning voice fills my ears.

"Are you feeling okay this morning?" he asks, his voice filled with concern.

"Yeah I am okay, but we have to get up, we have school today" I tell him pulling up out of his strong grip.

"But baby I want to stay in bed" he groans, pulling me back down.

"NO" I snap at him. "We are getting up and going to

school. Now I am going to have a shower, and you can go make me breakfast" I get up out of bed and stride over to my bathroom ignoring the fact I'm naked and the pain throbbing between my legs.

As I get into the bathroom I hear Zaid call out "Damn you're hot when you're angry". Ignoring him, I turn the shower on and let the hot water flow over my body, taking away the pain. Drying off, I slip on some lace underwear just to tease Zaid, a pair of tight black jeans with a red singlet top finishing with my black 'I hate Mondays' hoodie with my red converse.

Tying my hair up in a high ponytail I grab my bag with my phone and wallet and walk into the kitchen where I find chocolate and blueberry pancakes on the table with a hot looking Zaid still in the kitchen. As I sit down Zaid walks over and sits down with me placing a plate in front of the both of us.

"I hope you don't mind that I used the shower down the hall" he says, cutting up his pancakes.
"No, no, it's okay. I like the new clothes" I wink knowing he has found Anthony's old wardrobe.
"Sorry, next to the bathroom I found a bedroom full of guys' clothes and I guessed they were your brothers, so I decided I would borrow them unless you would like me to go to school naked?" he teases, making me almost choke on my pancake. "Don't worry I wouldn't do that. But we better get going".

Mollie's POV

After finishing our pancakes and putting the dishes in the dishwasher we leave for school.

"Hey Jemma" I call out to her as I see her near the school entrance.
"Monster!" she yells running at me giving me a massive hug. "I am guessing you and Zaid had a good night last night" she winks at me.
"SHUT UP!" I swat her arm away with an angry look.
"OMG YOU DID! Was he good? Is he big?" She fires questions at me.
"SHUT UP" I yell at her before storming off to my locker.

As I pull open my locker, a manila folder falls out. 'Stuff you Martin' is all I can think. I pull the books I need until lunch out and put them in a bag I keep in my locker. In a hurry, I rush off to class.

The bell for lunch rings and I run off to the cafe before anyone else. Making my way to the front towards the cash register I pay for my lunch and run off to a hidden part of the school to read over the files. Taking a seat and pulling the files out I read over them.

```
Name: James Anderson
Common Hang-Out: Luda Hotel
Location: Next to Luda Arcade
Deadline: Friday
```

Shit! That only leaves tonight, tomorrow and the next day. I don't know if I can keep doing this. If he wants me to keep doing this, Drew is going to have to give me a better reason and up the pay. Pulling out my phone I knew this call was something I had to do.

"Hey Drew speaking," he answers casually.
"We need to talk".
"Then speak".
"If you want me to continue this, then I need a better reason and you will need to up the pay".
"Aww sweetie are you threatening me?"
"I hate you, you sick bastard! Now give me a reason and up my pay"

"I have people at your mothers work watching her, there are also people at your sister's college watching her too. Jemma is here and I can deal with her. I am still waiting to track down that brother of yours" he warns me.
"GO ROT IN HELL YOU CRAZY LUNATIC!" I yell at him before I end the call. He is so getting on my nerves; I should just kill him instead. I stay there and finish my lunch before packing up my things and heading off to find my handsome boyfriend.

Walking into the classroom, I find Zaid sitting alone at the back. Happily, I skip over to him and take the empty seat on his right. Pulling out my books and placing them on the desk in front of me I lay my head on his shoulder.
"Hey Zaidy-Po," I whisper to him.
"Where were you at lunch?" He demands, turning to face me, knocking my head off his shoulder. He is clearly pissed.

Mollie's POV

"I-I-I was sitting alone in my 'hiding' place," I stutter out scared of what he might do. I edge away from him when he snaps at me again.

"YOU DITCHED ME!" he yells, not caring that there are other people in the room. "AFTER LAST NIGHT I THOUGHT YOU WOULD HAVE WANTED TO HAVE LUNCH WITH ME AT LEAST!"

"I'm sorry," I whisper, grabbing my books and stuffing them in my bag, not bothering to look down to hide my tears.

"WHAT THE HELL DO YOU THINK YOU'RE DOING?" he bellows as I stand up and run out of the class.

Running down the corridors of the school trying to see through my tears. I run until I find the janitors closet. Gripping the handle, I pull it open hard and fast, catching the couple inside by surprise. By the look on their faces, you can tell that they were scared of what I would do. In a hurry I watch them rush out and sprint off to class. Just as I shut the door another person pulls it open; this angers me. Can't people just leave me a one? Standing in the door frame is a concerned looking James. He pushes me into the room before shutting the door behind him.

"What do you want?" I ask in between sobs.

"Are you okay?" he dismisses my question leaving it unanswered.

"Yes I'm fine! What the hell does it look like!? Now answer my question," I snap at him pissed off and sobbing. "What do you want?"

"Just to make sure you were okay, Zaid was pissed when you skipped lunch," he tried to pull me into a hug, but I push him away.

"I know," I say, letting my eyes wander around the room, they land on a shelf that has knives beside me.

Slipping my hand out I clutch the knife behind my back as James is looking the other way. The glorious feeling of wanting to see blood washes over me. As quick as a flash I plunge the knife through his back into his heart killing him instantly, without a struggle. His body falls limp on the ground, blood pooling around him. Picking up a key to the room, hanging on a hook near the door, I walk out of the room, quickly locking it behind me.

Walking off I drop the key at the office desk, and begin the walk home. On the way home I decide to call Drew. "Hello," he answers. "What do you want now?"

"He's dead in the janitor's closet. Key is at the office desk unattended."

"You killed James today?" he questions, sounding shocked.

"Yes, now no more please," I say before hanging up. Arriving at my house I enter and lock the door behind me before running off to my room and collapsing on my bed, into an unsettled sleep.

Thunderous knocking on the front door wakes me from my slumber. Instantly I knew it wouldn't be my mother, as she would have let herself in. Not caring about what I look like I walk to the door and answer it.

"Hello," I hear a masculine voice say to me. I know I've heard that voice before, but I don't recognise the face.

"Did you miss me, baby sister?" the man asks.

"Anthony?" I ask not sure I believe It's him until he nods.

"ANTHONY!" I scream, wrapping my arms around him, giving him a massive hug. "Of course I missed you, you idiot," I laugh at him.

"Are we going to stand here and have you kill me with your tight hugs, or are you gonna let me in?" he asks with a grin on his face.

"I thought you'd like to stay on the doorstep all night," I chuckle, letting go of him. "Come in, Mother isn't home, she hasn't been lately."

I watch as Anthony walks into the living room and dumps his bags by the couch. "Nothing has changed since I was here last," he states, sitting down on the couch. "Come sit next to me and tell me about this boyfriend of yours," he says, patting the space next to him. Taking the seat next to him he pulls me into him, holding me in a hug.

"What do you want to know about him?"

"How about his name first?" he asks.

"His name is Zaid Yousuf and he's in the all-boys singing group Jemma likes," I says snuggling into him. I miss having my brother to comfort me.

"Huh well okay. I have one question to ask you, okay baby sis?"

"Fire away."

You Make Me Crazy

"Have you guys been doing the dirty?" I look at him shocked!

"Wow my little sister is doing the dirty with a famous guy!" he laughs at my embarrassment.
"Shut up Anthony I never said that!" I huff, crossing my arms.
"Moo, you didn't have to, I called Jemma and after 'hello' it was the first thing she told me."
"That traitor," I grumble, getting up stomping around the room.
"Calm down sis. She only told me that because you left school before Fifth Period class. She was worried about you, that's all."

"Well, I'm sorry if no one knows about what's been happening to me; that my boyfriend yelled at me just because I wasn't with him at lunch!" I feel my voice rising with each word until I am screaming the last part.
"Okay!" he yells back at me. "Why did he yell at you?" he asks as we both calmed down.

"He said he thought I ditched him after last night, he also thought I would be attached to him at lunch," I mumble out hoping my brother would think nothing of it.
"HE WHAT!" he exclaims, jumping out of his seat. "I'll come back later," before I can stop him he rushes out of the door, to his car and drives off. Looking at the time I notice it is getting late, so I make myself dinner and go.

Zaid's POV

"This is the last one right?" I hear Mollie ask them the rustle of paper and the opening of a desk drawer. There is a noise at a window then I hear a male voice,
"Yes, it is. Unless you want more, and if you do then you know where to find me." After hearing that, I turn and walk back to the kitchen. I know something is going on, something that my girlfriend isn't telling me.
"She will be out soon" I tell Jemma and Drew to sit down at the table "Let's start."

"There you are monster! I thought you fell asleep," Jemma says, if only she knew who she was meeting with, if only I knew.
"Ha! It totally looks like you all waited for me before eating" her voice is full of sarcasm.
"Sorry Mollie" I say not noticing that I am talking quieter than usual. We all finish dinner in a slightly uncomfortable silence.

After dinner I decide I need to find out what is going on with Mollie. "Excuse me, I need to go to the bathroom" I say standing up and leaving the table.

You Make Me Crazy

Quietly I walk down the hallway to Mollie's room and open the door, closing it behind me. Looking around I see her desk over in the corner.

Without moving anything on her messy bedroom floor, I carefully walk over to her desk. Reaching out my arm, my hand grips the handle of the lower draw pulling open, I see nothing but pens and pencils. Closing the drawer, I move up and open the middle one, it is full of what looked like school books. I open the top desk draw and find nothing; it is completely empty. Making sure I've left everything as it was I walk back out of her room closing the door behind me and out to the kitchen.

Drew's POV

As I enter her room I feel that we are being spied on, someone is eavesdropping at the door. The only thoughts that are going through my mind is that I know Mollie wouldn't complete her final task and I will have to hurt innocent people so this will get done.

As soon as I arrive, I leave again, whoever is at the door, will have the courage to find the files. I stand outside her window hidden in the shadows until she leaves her room. Standing there watching, I see she has left. Quickly I sneak back in and grab the files out of her draw and stuff them under her mattress.

Looking up I notice her phone is on her bed. Picking it up I find that it is lock.
"Fuck!" I cry out silently in frustration. I try the simplest code I can think of, 5674. "Wow," I whisper, "I got it!" I look and find her reminders and set a buzzer to go off an hour from now, 7pm.

I hear footsteps approaching and drop her phone, quickly jumping out the window. Just before leaving her property, I see Zaid walk into her room and over to her desk. Thank god I moved the files before he found them, I wouldn't want him leaving her just yet.

Mollie's POV

F inally they leave, it feels like it's been hours seeing that the whole night Zaid kept quiet and didn't make conversation with me. I walk into my room, "bleep, bleep, bleep, bleep," I hear my phone ring. Rushing over to my bed I pick it up, a notification? I never set a notification for anything, or did I?

I look at the notification
/the files are under your mattress. DM/
WHAT?! DREW HAS BEEN IN MY ROOM AGAIN? AND HE GOT PAST MY CODE? URGH I HATE THIS BASTARD!

Lifting my mattress, I find the files and move them onto my bed. Sitting down I pull out my new manilla folder and open it.

Name: Zaid Yousuf
Hangout: With you
Location: Anywhere you are
Deadline: One week from today
Note: If you fail to do this, BAD things will start happening, now I know where your brother is

Oh shit! I can't kill my own boyfriend; I just can't do it. NO! I jump up off my bed and run to the bathroom. Head

74

over to the toilet bowl and I hurl up my insides, I vomit non-stop until there is nothing left to bring up. Brushing it off as shock I get up and brush my teeth.

"Mollie, Molls, are you okay?" Anthony calls out running to the bathroom.
"Yeah I'm okay Ant, I just have a tummy bug," I say while walking into his outstretched arms.
"Would you like me to walk you to bed and get you a glass of water?"
"It's okay, I'll just go to sleep, I have school tomorrow. Don't worry big brother," I walk through to my room and hop into the bed.
Looking up at the doorway I see his silhouette standing there. "Lil sis, I'm leaving early tomorrow. I have some people to see. I will be back when you get home okay?"
"Okay" I yawn. "Goodnight. I love you big brother."

A month later

Letting my eyes flutter open, I look around my surroundings, I'm still in my bedroom. In an urgent wish, I spring from my bed and head over to the toilet bowl, I throw up again. Damn this tummy bug is still here.
"Anthony!" I yell for my brother before remembering he isn't home, and my mother hasn't been home for over a week. "Urgh!" I get up and walk to the home phone in the kitchen and call school saying that I will be off today sick. Crawling back into bed I hear my phone chime.

From Jemma:

You Make Me Crazy

```
Where are you? I didn't see
you this morning. Are you ok?
```

To Jemma:

```
I have a tummy bug, see
you tomorrow.
```

It chimes again. Urgh! Stupid phone!

From Zaid:

```
Hey baby x Sorry about last
night. Jemma said you had
a tummy bug, did you want me
to come around after school?
```

To Zaid:

```
No but thanks and it's okay.
```

Finally, I can sleep.

4 hours later

Stretching my arms out above my head I sit up and glance over at the clock, 12:34 pm. Wow! I slept past lunch. Getting up off my bed I grip hold of my head board to steady me, why do I feel so dizzy and sick? I walk into the kitchen and open the fridge, hmm what to eat? What to eat?

All of a sudden I see chocolate sauce with fresh carrots next to it. Oh, how I'm craving carrot and chocolate sauce. Taking them out of the fridge and pouring the sauce into a small bowl, I pick up a kitchen knife and cut the carrot in to stick snack size pieces. Picking up the dishes I take a seat at the table. 'Oh, damn these tastes good!' I thought.

Just as I put the last of it all in my mouth and swallow. I jump up and rush to the toilet, throwing up again. 'I think this is more than a tummy bug' looking at the clock I see it would be lunch break at school. I'll call Heather and see if she can pop around and see me. Getting my phone off my bedside table, I call her.

"Hello Heather speaking" she answers professional y.
"Hey cousin, it's me. Mollie"
"Hey, are you okay? I didn't see you at school today".
"Can you come and see me while you are on your lunch break?" I ask.
"Yeah sure I can do that cousin. Want me to get you anything?"
"Yeah can you please get me a pregnancy test?"
"Okay, but I only hope for your sake that it is negative"
"Thank you. See you soon". Just as I am about to hang up I remember we are now out of carrots. "Oh, and can you get me some carrots?"

You Make Me Crazy

She laughs at me! "Sure, be there in ten minutes" Then she hangs up.

Ten minutes later, she knocks at the door. I manage to drag myself off the couch and over to it to let her in. "Okay Mollie, go take the test and I will put the carrots in the fridge" Heather hands the test over to me and walks into the kitchen with the carrots.

Walking to the bathroom my hands start to shake with nerves. I really hope it's negative. I wait five minutes like the instructions say, then nervously took a look. It's....it's....it's positive! Just as I read it, I faint.

Heather's POV

Heather's POV

A fter hearing a loud thump, I run to the bathroom to see if Mollie is okay. Finding Mollie's unconscious body on the floor, I spy the test lying on the counter. Picking it up, I see that it says positive.

"Oh shit!" I exclaim, just as Anthony walks down the hallway.

"Hey Heather. Why are you here?" He asks me, slightly confused but happy to see me. I hold up the test so he can see the positive sign.

"You're pregnant?!" He exclaims excitedly.

"No" I say looking back at Mollie. "Mollie is."

"She is?" he asks, stunned.

"I guess she found out and then fainted. I need you to move her off the bathroom floor and onto her bed for me please." I ask him calmly.

"Ah... sure okay." He picks her up gently and places her on her bed. "Does her boyfriend know?"

"She just found out. We are the only three who know. Let her tell him in her own time."

"Urgh! Fine but I have to at least tell mum and Sylv a."

"I'll call aunty, and you call your sister."

Anthony's POV

How on earth is my little sister pregnant? PREGNANT! Now I have to call Sylvia and tell her.

"Hey Sylvia, it's Anthony."

"Oh hey bro what's up"

"Nothing really. When are you coming home again?"

"In a year sadly"

"You will want to be back sooner, Aunty Sylvia."

"Aunty Sylvia?... Wait, did you get a girl pregnant?

"No. Mollie is"

"What!" She shrieks. "Are you kidding me? Is this a joke?"

"No it's not April fools, you can even ask cousin Heather. She brought her the test."

"I'll see when I can come back. It might take a month."

"That's okay, I'll tell her you say hello and you're disappointed."

"Thank you Ant. Talk soon."

Mollie's POV

M y head is pounding, rolling over and I open my eyes. Sitting at the end of my bed I see my darling brother and favourite cousin.

"Are you okay now Mollie?"

"Yes I guess I am. It wasn't a dream was it?" I ask them.

"No it wasn't. But I hope you know this is your responsibility now." Anthony says sadly, sounding a little disappointed with me.

"What's the time?" I ask tiredly.

"It's five pm." They answer in unison.

"Can Zaid come over so I can tell him?" I ask nervously,

"Sure, Heather is going to head home now. She came back once she finished work." Anthony answers.

"Thank you cuz" I say, giving her a hug as she and Anthony leave my room.

Picking up my phone, turning it on, and unlocking it to call Zaid.

"Hey Zaid, it's Mollie"

"Hey, are you feeling okay?"

"Can you come over as soon as possible?" I ask to avoid his question.

"I'll be there in 20 minutes then. Want me to get you anything?"

"No it's okay thank you."

You Make Me Crazy

After hanging up my phone I fall deep into thought. I
don't want my child to grow up without a father, I can't
murder Zaid. I need to tell him about Martin's deals.
Also, I have to tell Drew that it needs to stop!
Picking up my phone I send Drew a text

To Drew The Crazy Lunatic:

```
It's over! I'm not doing
this anymore.
```

Within seconds he replies back but this time with an
attachment. Before reading the message I open the
attachment and save it to my phone. The photo is taken
in a basement, it is of a woman, but not just any woman.
The woman is my mother. Sitting there hands bound by
ropes looking beaten and bruised. I scroll down and look
at the message.

From Drew:

```
SHE WILL BE DEAD IN THREE
DAYS. IF YOU WANT HER ALIVE
YOU WILL DO IT.
```

I must tell Zaid and Anthony. Maybe they can help me
find a way to fix this situation. I hear a knock at the front
door. Zaid is here. Getting up off my bed I walk towards
the front where Anthony and Zaid are standing next to
each other, Anthony sporting a scowl.

"You okay monster?" Zaid asks me. "I came over as soon as you called."

Staring at him I didn't know what to tell him. "I'm fine but we need to talk." Looking at him as his face drops. He can only be thinking the worst thing now; that I am going to break up with him.
"Oh...um...okay" he responds, his voice trembling while tears begin to form.
"You two can go talk in the lounge. I will be in my room" Anthony says leaving the room.

Zaid and I walk into the lounge and take a seat on opposite couches.
"What did you want to talk about?" he asks me, staring down at his hands that rest in his lap.
"I'm pregnant" I blurt out.
"Is it mine?" He looks up at me with a hopeful expression on his face.
"Yes, it is," I respond, looking down at my hands.

"That's fantastic to hear Mollie. I'm so happy for us. But why do you look so sad and upset?" He moves so he is sitting next to me wrapping his arms around me.
"I need your help with something and also you are going to hate me for it." I let silent tears fall down my face.
"Then tell me, please".
"Anthony needs to hear this too, as it involves him as much as it does you".
"ANTHONY WE NEED YOU HERE!" He yells down the hallway and that brings him running to my aid.

You Make Me Crazy

"Is he rejecting it being his? Is he hurting you? Are you ok? Do I need to beat him up?" Anthony quickly fires questions at me.

"I need to talk to you both about something. It's really important, and you are both going to hate me for it" I say standing up. "I just have to pick up something from my room". I quickly run up to my room and grab the files. Running back to the lounge I dump the files on the coffee table in front of the boys.

"What are these?" Anthony asks, pointing at them.
"Shut up and let me talk" I snap at him.
Opening all the folders on the table they both lean forward to look at them. There are five files and one of the targets is still alive.

"I turned into an assassin. Drew Martin paid me to do it, to kill all the guys of Four Singers and a Casket, no matter who they were dating. The only reason I continued to do it is because he threatened to harm Sylvia, Mom and Anthony, also Heather. The last task was to kill Zaid. I received it last night. I refused to do it, and he sent me a picture of my mother - our mother sorry Anthony, and she is bound by rope in a basement and has been beaten and looks of bruise marks are visible. I regret all the murders but there is one that I won't regret and that is Martins. Also, before the first one he sent me to a place to pick up a black duffle bag full of weapons - I have only used a few." I tell them worrying about what they are going to say.

Mollie's POV

"Where is mom? I don't care that you murdered four guys because you did it to protect your family and future family. We need to find mom and dispose of Drew whatever it takes." Anthony says.

"He threatened your family!" Zaid begins, "I don't care, he wanted me dead, but he threatened people I love so he could get who he wanted killed."

"Monster, don't worry, we will help you kill him. Can you show us the bag of weapons?" Anthony asks cautiously. Nervously I nod. I never actually looked through it properly myself. Together the three of us walk to my bedroom. Bending over I pull the bag out.

Putting the bag on my bed I open it and empty out the contents.

Knives
Nunchucks
Rope
Wire
Machete
Sniper
Shotgun
Pistol

"Wow! That's a lot of weapons!" Anthony says in what seems to be awe. "I see that only the knives, rope and nunchucks have been used".

"Well yeah" I sit down on the ground holding my head in my hands.

You Make Me Crazy

"Hey it's going to be okay" Zaid says sitting down next to me pulling me into his lap and holding me tight.
"He said you had to be dead by the end of the week" I whimper. "Drew's going to hurt mum otherwise, then Heather, Sylvia and Anthony. We can't let him find out about the baby either or he could try to harm it" traitorous tears ran down my face.

I watch as Anthony packs all the weapons back into the bag and slid it back under my bed.
"Come on Mollie, go have a nap or you will stress out the baby. Zaid can lie with you if you want" Anthony suggests, pulling back my bed covers so I can get in.
"Anthony is right Mollie, we need to start thinking about our baby," Zaid agrees kissing my head.

"Yeah you're right I guess. I'm feeling tired." With that I climb into my bed with Zaid gently wrapping his arms around me.

Anthony's POV

I stay quiet as I walk into the park, nothing but empty openness around me. No trees, no plants, no playground. Looking up, I see Drew walking towards me, I have asked him to meet me here. I told him, I wanted to talk to him about a recording contract, but actually I have something else planned.
"I didn't know you were musical" Drew says smugly.
I don't care about what he has to say. This guy's foul mouth won't get him anywhere in my world, he can't talk himself out of anything.

Walking close enough so I am next to him, I ball up my fists. Planting my feet in a fighting stance, my fist meets his face, breaking his jaw and shattering his teeth, that was expected with the stealth speed I put the knuckle busters on with.
"What the fuck was that for?!" he yells clutching his face in pain
"That is for what you have put my little sister through you arrogant asshole!" I spit at him.
Grasping his upper arms, I pull him up, so he is standing and drag him into an alleyway. Just as we get there, Mollie runs out of nowhere making me lose my grip on the bastard.

"Stop Anthony! Leave him," she shouts at me making me drop him to the ground. Mollie bends down to his level to see if he is okay. "Go away Anthony" she turns to me. Knowing that if I don't do what she asks I will be living in hell I turn and walk away.

Mollie's POV

"What the fuck was that for!?" I hear Drew yell out. I run from where I am hiding and see Drew clutching his face while Anthony stands in a fighting position.

"That was for what you have put my little sister through you arrogant asshole" Anthony yells at him picking him up and walking into an alleyway.

"Stop Anthony! Leave him" I shout, making Drew drop to the ground. I bend down to see if he is okay, he has a broken jaw and is spitting out shattered teeth. "Go away Anthony" I say watching him turn and walk away.

"Are you okay Drew?" I ask. He stands and pulls me further into the alleyway. He pins me up against the wall and yanks down my pants taking my underwear with them.

I let out a high pitch scream as the cold air touches my parts.

"Stop Drew," I scream. He holds me up with one arm and uses the other hand to open his pants and bring out his small four-inch dick.

"NO!" I scream again. But he doesn't stop. He forces my legs apart holding me up so I can't escape. Just as he aligns himself with my entrance he falls on the ground, pulling me down with him. My mouth lands near his dick. Pushing himself up on his elbows he tries moving his

89

hips into my open mouth, seeing what he is trying to do, I reach down to my pocket and pull out my knife.

Watching the shiny blade cut through his penis, I feel hands pull me away from his semi unconscious body. Looking behind me, I see Zaid helping me with a sniper on a nearby rooftop. I watch as Zaid walks over to him and begins kicking him in the face. I double over feeling sick as I hear the bones in his face break.

Together, Zaid and I walk out from the alleyway, hearing sirens and seeing police cars come down the street. Anthony walks up to us and helps me over to a seat. Where I sit being hugged by my two favourite guys who have recently helped me a lot.

Epilogue

P icking up the tray of coffee, cookies and cut up slices of chocolate covered fruit, I walk into the lounge of mine and Zaid's new house. Placing the tray on our mahogany coffee table I take our two-year-old baby girl out of my loving husband's arms.

I was never charged with anything for the murders, but I had to go to counselling for a long time. Anthony has taken up a job working at the prison where Drew is currently being kept under lock and key. Somehow he managed to find out about our daughter and promised he would get her one day.

"Honey stop thinking about it okay" Zaid says pulling our little darling and I into his arms.
"Okay I'll try, I just hope we can keep her safe" I pick up my coffee slowly taking a sip.
"We will. Don't worry" He reassures me.

Acknowledgements

The editing & formatting crew, Chloe King & Kasashaa Scott.

My Little sister, Mollie, for the inspiration to originally draft this and the motivation to make it her eighteenth birthday present. In addition, forever being a reminder that if you egg me on enough to do something, I will make it happen.

Other Books By Author

2025

The Edited Collection

Poetry inspired by those who have come into my life and events that occurred. Though some of their stories in my journey were short, others have lasted a lifetime. Dedicated to those who fought their hardest battles and concurred their own evils within.

Written Works of Friends

Primed for Failure
<u>Chloe King</u>

A collection of 17 short stories, most with a horror/thriller element to them. Read them if you dare, for some twisted tales await you inside.

The Roses Series
<u>Kasashaa Scott</u>

Recently returned from court after the death of her mother, Elizabeth Ayton becomes a lady in waiting for the Queen of England. It soon becomes clear that she has captured the attention of a persistent admirer, the King of England. After becoming the Kings hidden mistress against her own wishes, she will have to make some tough choices if she wishes to keep control of her life.